Cornelius

Copyright © 1983 by Leo Lionni

All rights reserved. Published in the United States by Dragonfly Books, an imprint of Random House
Children's Books, a division of Random House, Inc., New York. Originally published in hardcover in
the United States by Pantheon Books, a division of Random House, Inc., New York, in 1983.

Dragonfly Books with the colophon is a registered trademark of Random House, Inc.

Visit us on the Web! www.randomhouse.com/kids

Educators and librarians, for a variety of teaching tools, visit us at www.randomhouse.com/teachers

Library of Congress Cataloging-in-Publication Data is available upon request.
ISBN 978-0-679-86040-2 (pbk.)

MANUFACTURED IN CHINA

23 22 21 20 19 18

Random House Children's Books supports the First Amendment and celebrates the right to read.

Cornelius

a fable by Leo Lionni

Dragonfly Books  New York

When the eggs hatched,
the little crocodiles crawled out
onto the riverbeach.
But Cornelius walked out *upright*.

As he grew taller and stronger
he rarely came down on all fours.
He saw things no other
crocodile had ever seen before.
"I can see far beyond the bushes!"
he said.
But the others said,
"What's so good about that?"

"I can see the fish from above!" Cornelius said.
"So what?" said the others, annoyed.

And so one day, Cornelius angrily decided to walk away.

It was not long before he met a monkey.
"I can walk upright!" Cornelius said proudly.
"And I can see things far away!"

"I can stand on my head," said the monkey.

"And hang from my tail."
Cornelius was amazed. "Could I learn to do that?" he asked.

"Of course," replied the monkey.
"All you need is a lot of hard work
and a little help."

Cornelius worked hard
at learning the monkey's tricks,
and the monkey seemed happy
to help him.

When he had finally learned to stand on his head
and hang from his tail,
Cornelius walked proudly back to the riverbeach.

"Look!" he said. "I can stand on my head."
"So what!" was all the others said.

"And I can hang from my tail!"
said Cornelius.
But the others
just frowned and repeated,
"So what!"

Disappointed and angry,
Cornelius decided to go back to the monkey.
But just as he had turned around, he looked back.
And what did he see?

There the others were, falling all over themselves
trying to stand on their heads and hang from their tails!
Cornelius smiled. Life on the riverbeach
would never be the same again.

About the Author

Leo Lionni, an internationally known designer, illustrator, and graphic artist, was born in Holland and studied in Italy until he came to the United States in 1939. He was the recipient of the 1984 American Institute of Graphic Arts Gold Medal and was honored posthumously in 2007 with the Society of Illustrators Lifetime Achievement Award. His picture books are distinguished by their enduring moral themes, graphic simplicity, and brilliant use of collage, and include four Caldecott Honor Books: *Inch by Inch*, *Frederick, Swimmy,* and *Alexander and the Wind-Up Mouse.* Hailed as "a master of the simple fable" by the *Chicago Tribune,* he died in 1999 at the age of 89.